TRUE ANIMAL STORIES

by Stedman H. Carr, D.V.M.

dr. ball
BOUNCING BALL BOOKS
"From the Florida Swamp to Readers Everywhere"

True Animal Stories

written and illustrated
by Stedman H. Carr, D.V.M.

Copyright Library of Congress 2005
Bouncing Ball Books
All Rights Reserved

Registration TXu-1-208-180
ISBN 80-902746-2-5
EAN 978-80-902746-2-4

Short Stories by Stedman H. Carr, D.V.M.
"True Animal Stories" 2006

Novel by Stedman H. Carr, D.V.M.
"Maria, Me, And Animals" second printing 2006
"CW and Me" 2006
"Animal Sleuths: From Doc's Mystery Files" 2007

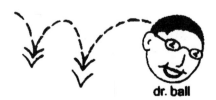

dr. ball

www.bouncingballbooks.com

DEDICATION

-For all those who share and value the human-animal bonding relationship.

INTRODUCTION

I am a retired veterinarian.

These are some animal stories that I uniquely remember after many years of practice.

I wish to share them with you.

TWENTY-TWO STORIES

Snowball Snowflake

Hobo

Forensic Poodle

Fearless Teddy

Two Cats

Gal And Guy

Tippy

Prozac The FID

Lancelot's Castles

Swissy From Switzerland

Her Royal Highness's Business

Kachina Dolls

The Studly

Daniel Webster

Faith And Calvin

Torque

Mafia Cat

King The Grocery King

Coughing Little Bit

Midnight Holloween

Daiquiri

Bingo The Therapy Cat

SNOWBALL... SNOWFLAKE

Snowball was a smallish, white, fluffy American Eskimo Dog. Her life was one of ease and entertainment. She had learned to answer to *Snowball* for Mrs., *Snowflake* for Mr., and as an aside *Be Still* for the groomer.

Snowball liked to adventure. The ride to and from the groomer was part of her entertainment. She interacted with other vehicles and made clever pantomimes, especially at passing children. The weekly Dog Park trip was even more fun, but she felt left out with the Frisbee crowd. She wanted to be a participant, not a spectator. However, she was not amused as she road to the animal hospital. About a mile before, and just at the exit off the expressway, she would start to drool. Then she would lick her lips and vomit. Different medications for nausea, motion sickness, anxieties, and even sedations were tried. All were a total failure. The other trips were part of an adventure, in which the Dog Park had the best rating. She rated it a "10." The groomer was rated an "8" because of the other dogs.

The animal hospital trip was a "-10." The barf bag around her neck helped somewhat, but it seemed to be quite an embarrassment. She sat quietly with her head down out of view from other passer-byers. She learned to swallow most of the barf. Food was withheld. The spit-up was now white foamy phlegm. Since this was a trip every six months the puking caper was accepted as a necessary evil, and the park continued to be a weekly treat.

She watched the Frisbee tosses intently. She was jealous. Her pay attention bark was a, *"Yip, Yip!"* Now she yipped and yipped, and added a whine as she looked at the Frisbees sailing in the air. On the next park trip there were two Frisbees just for her. She quickly learned to catch and when she missed, she would fetch it back. This influenced her time at home from being more sedate to game playing. She would pick up stuff around the apartment and deposit it on the coffee table in a fetch and retrieve style. It was playtime!

It was not long before Mr. and Mrs. begin to hide toys for her to find and retrieve to the coffee table. Then followed hide and seek. Snowflake would yip-yip at Mrs. and run into a bedroom and hide. One of her favorite places to hide was under a blanket at the foot of the bed. Her black nose stuck out, but her eyes were covered so she thought that she was invisible.

Mrs. would come in and say, "Where is Snowball? Snowball. . . Snowball come out where ever you are. Where is Snowball? Come out from hidey!"

She repeated this several times. Then she would start a mock search until . . .

"There she is!"

The only flaw in the entertainment relationship was the vet/vomit trip. This was overlooked. One Sunday Mr. was changing his shoelaces. Snowflake came over to investigate. Mr. started a game. He dangled a shoelace and teased with jerking motions. Snowflake reacted by trying to catch the string, but it would be jerked out of reach just as she snapped. The game was fun in a way. Finally Snowflake decided to end the game mostly because she was tired of being called Flakey, i.e. Snowflake. She caught the shoelace and quickly swallowed it.

It was a rush to the animal hospital and the emergency room. Dread results were imaginedA blockage followed by surgery! A stomach puncture followed by shock! Snowflake enjoyed the ride. Mr. took a short cut. He kept urging Snowflake to vomit.

"Snowflake we are going to the vet. Listen up. Don't be flakey. I apologize. From now on I will call you Snowball. Pay attention. V.E.T! That spells vet. Horrible needles and sticking black things down your ears! **And** remember the glove up the butt. Puke! Vomit! Barf! Hey, I will never call you Snowflake again! You are not flakey. Just get sick, please!"

Snowball sat and looked out the window. There was not even a drool. She seemed happy to have captured the shoelace. She had won the game and was now content. She was flaky no more.

Mr. thought, "She always barfs on the way to the vet. Why not now? What is different? This is not the normal way I go. She doesn't know this way. That's why! O.K. Back we go to square one, and then off to the vet!"

Mr. backtracked and started the regular route. At the enter ramp to the expressway the drooling started. At the exit ramp to the animal hospital Snowflake, now Snowball, vomited up the shoelace. She settled down as Mr. U-turned and went back home. Mrs. collected all the items that could be swallowed. She Snowball-proofed the apartment.

"Snowball . . . Snowball, it is hidey time."

HOBO

Hobo was a male blue-eyed white cat. He was physically big boned and composed mostly of muscle. Mentally, he was serene and contemplative. He did not know a permanent name because he had been called many. Hobo is simply a designated name that reflects his life style.

He went from place to place on his own accord; that is, whenever the mood occurred. On occasion, he would stay a few months in one place. He did not roam about, but hitched a ride to new adventures.

The new people who adopted him had to meet certain criteria. They had to be caring, but not mushy-kissy. Mutual respect was mandatory. Certain basics such as entertainment, time out, good food, and naps were required.

Now, he was on the road once more. He was going away from the college and the student boarding house that had adopted him. They called him, Socrates, because he paid attention to the one talking; then turned to another in order to listen. He got opinions from all. "A Socratic way of teaching," so the students thought.

George was nervous as he dressed for the interview. He chose black loafers, khaki pants, white shirt, red tie, and a blue jacket. His apartment was student-small. Then he took his valise with his resume, breath freshener, and Grey Flannel splash on and headed to the parking lot. The interview was for a job that he was prepared for and now that he had his MBA, he felt ready. There would be many applicants with as good as or better than his academic records, so he thought he needed to look confident. He wished to be erudite, be committed, and be a good communicator. Finally, he thought he was having a breakdown. He had to keep his right hand in his jacket pocket because when he became nervous, he tended to pull his ear lobe.

Getting seated in his car, he noticed that he was not wearing a tie tack. He rushed back into the apartment and left the car window down. Hobo was watching from underneath an Indian Hawthorn bush. His nomadic impulse needed sating, so he leapt through the car window and settled under the seat to wait for the next happening.

George selected a silver tie tack to match the buttons of his silver jacket and off he went to the office complex. He arrived at the parking lot and drove around until he found a visitor's parking space located next to a reserved section. He locked the car and as he was putting on his jacket, a gray BMW zipped into the reserved space.

Lisa popped out and stepped behind George's car. Hobo was staring out the rear window.

"Sir, you should not lock a cat in a car. He will die of heat stroke."

"What cat?"

"That cat! You know, the one looking at us."

"Well, I don't own a cat."

"Well, he is in your vehicle. See."

"How do you know that he is a he?"

"He is jowly! Should be neutered! We need to control the cat population."

"Look, I'll move the car to a shady spot and crack the windows. I have an appointment in twenty minutes. Then I'll find out about the cat. Maybe he has a tag."

"Fine. I hope your meeting is a short one."

George moved the car, cracked the windows, and Hobo sat and watched. The office directory listed: **Dr. L. Ensley - 542, 5th Floor**. George waited in the reception area. Shortly thereafter, he was ushered into Dr. Ensley's office. She was the one in the parking lot!

"Please be seated. Moved your car?"

"Sure, everything is fine. Nice cat."

"What is the boy's name?"

"The cat?"

"Yes."

George noticed a used cheese wrapper thrown away in the wastebasket with the words, **"Tofu - Mozzarella Cheese Flavor"** on it. He did not know what Tofu was or how to pronounce it, and so he pulled on his right ear.

"Uh, his name is...I'll spell it, T.O.F.U."

"Tofu! How clever! You are to be congratulated. I'm a veggie myself."

George realized that he was in a hole and only digging it deeper. There was an exchange of niceties as Dr. Ensley scanned through the resume.

"Looks great! Start in two weeks. Some things we need to go over. How about a veggie brunch here? Then you get Tofu back home."

And so Hobo was the catalyst that started a relationship, albeit on false premises. Before the relationship was finalized Hobo moved on. Why? He was mostly ignored. It was always George and Lisa, Lisa and George. Also, his diet was strange. Soymilk? What is Tofu? Didn't they hear his stomach growling? Environmentally correct cat litter?

As Hobo walked away, only he knew the real reason. He heard whispers that all cats should be neutered or spayed.

FORENSIC POODLE

I was monitoring the pulse rate and oxygen blood level of Buddy, a dog, while the technician was doing a dental *prophy*. He was a small black poodle whose breath was becoming socially unacceptable. He had early gingivitis.

The technician said, "Hey Doc, seems to be some confusion with this dental chart. Check it out. Class one gingivitis, but no other problems."

Her work exceeded a "10" and his teeth looked great. "Looks good to me, your normal greatness," I said.

"Now look at Buddy's past dental chart. There should be a slab fracture repair of the fourth upper right premolar. No see?"

"I don't see it either. Could the charts be mixed up? Wrong dog? Have them check it out up front and scan the computer for breed, age, sex, name, and all that computer stuff."

I am not in charge of the computer work. Computer stuff to me was one of my rules: ***The A B C's***-A: plug it in, B: turn it on, and C: delegate; besides, micromanaging leads to burn-out. The staff was usually much better than me.

On my desk the next morning was Buddy's chart with a post-it-note and on it was a question mark. I opened the chart. There was a bold black permanent marker line drawn to separate the previous dental work. I compared last year's records to yesterday's chart. "Strange." The charts were different. "Let me see." It was the correct breed, age, sex and color, yet the dental charts were completely different. The owners name had been changed. The previous owner was Marilyn, but her name had been crossed out and now it reads *William.* The little poodle used to be named Zorro, and now, he was named Buddy.

I asked Julie up front to track down Marilyn. The next day Julie told me that Marilyn's apartment manager said that Marilyn had moved out a year ago and that some guy helped her move. He paid all of her rent so everything was kosher. She left no forwarding address. The apartment manager said that Marilyn had the sweetest little black poodle and they let her take him by the pool with his own little umbrella. His name was Zorro.

"Julie, try mailing her another reminder card!" I said, but there was no forwarding address.

I was busy and forgot about it until Janet came in with her cat for vaccinations. Janet asked me if Marilyn had come into the clinic lately because she had not seen her for several months. The women knew each other from work. Janet was the CPA for the Ramada Inn where Marilyn was the receptionist. Janet did not know where to send Marilyn W2 form.

"Let me see… Different dog no doubt!" I thought to myself. "Dental charts don't change! Was Marilyn a missing person?" I called the Tampa police.

"Yes!" She was missing and the case had gone cold. They had no leads until now. They would be right over.

William, the owner of Buddy, was arrested. He confessed and led them to the bodies of Marilyn and Zorro for a plea of some kind of murder that got him thirty years.

The story was that Marilyn and William met when they were both walking their dogs. The dogs came from the same litter and a conversation followed about the odds of such a coincidence. Then a date and finally they became lovers. "I don't understand why William would do such a thing. Commit murder to end an affair?" I thought.

When I don't understand I resort to astrophysics. For example, dark matter is something that is not there to explain something that makes no sense.

The dental records were enough to start an investigation and supply the name of the killer. He was caught because of a dog's dental records. Buddy/Zorro's dental charts were forensic evidence.

"How dumb is dumb? Dumb conjugated is still dumb. Dumb, dumber, dumbest!" William had given his name, address, and phone number when he checked Buddy into the clinic and tried to pass him off as Zorro.

I suspect that Buddy/Zorro's dental records are the only legally admitted canine forensic dental evidence in a murder in Florida.

FEARLESS TEDDY

Teddy was the normal "pocket rocket" Jack Russell Terrier. He could have been the inspiration for the "**No Fear**" t-shirt or the mascot for mountain climbers, sky divers, cave divers, and special operation forces - Navy Seals, Army Rangers, Delta Force, and the P-Js air rescue teams. Teddy would have never been in the Spy Ops who disseminate disinformation or propaganda and sit around in air-conditioned chat rooms drinking green tea. Even though that is important work, it was just not Teddy. He really did not contemplate much.

Although there had been, but never would there be again a situation that he feared. Except one time when it almost cost him his life, but that did not even register.

That one time Teddy and his human companion, a retired government worker from the Department of Treasury, were walking in a small park in the "over-the-hill" condo village in Florida. It restricted pet owners to dogs that weighed less than twenty pounds, and Teddy weighed twenty-three pounds. More or less, he was all muscle so even though he looked twenty pounds, he was registered as 10.5 kilograms on the paper work that no one ever bothered to convert to pounds.

The retired Mrs. was lonely; her husband died and she sold her Virginia home and came to Florida for retirement. It was not too long before she became attached to a neighbor's dog, Teddy the Jack Russell Terrier. She visited her neighbor in order to visit with Teddy, and as her neighbor had become more and more infirm, she became the caretaker of both Teddy and her. Then, after her neighbor died, she adopted Teddy.

Teddy was not named after the cuddly toy teddy bear, but its namesake, the fearless, imperialistic president Theodore Roosevelt. Because of Teddy, she, a retired introvert, was quite happy in her retirement. They were constant companions.

Twice daily they walked along the edge of the development that had a designated green space that was landscaped in native plants. They both enjoyed the walks. She with her tripod cane and Teddy leashed to a loosely fitting collar with all his tags attached. He examined all the greenery and went before her like a forward observer sweeping back and forth to check everything out. He never pulled the leash; for he was her protector.

The park-walkway was adjacent to a cow pasture; indeed, the retirement complex had been part of an old Florida "cracker" ranch. The grandchildren were selling off some acres every few years and kept a few cows to stay in the category of a ranch for tax purposes under the *Florida Green Belt* law.

The ranch-hand was elderly and beyond being a hand at anything; in fact, he could not even get on a horse anymore, but he wanted to stay and was the only one of the original family that had been the ranch-hands for three generations. He had Social Security and Medicare, so the heirs kept him and bought him an all-terrain vehicle (ATV). He was there more for a presence. His job was sort of security, knowing fully that he could not secure anything.

He would drive his ATV with his shotgun in a holster around the fence daily and stop and talk to the people looking at the cows. He wore his old brimmed up sweat stained straw hat, jeans and western attire including boots. He was the last of a dying breed and would be damned if he was going to change, and his boots would be on as he lay in his coffin. However, he had to give up snuff because it gave him diarrhea and pyorrhea.

The people he talked to all said, "Please don't sell the land! It is so nice to have open space with cows and birds; plus, it's so peaceful."

"How dumb!" He thought. "Here they have come into a restricted gated condo all with the same floor plan that was once part of the ranch and now they wanted to keep others out."

In a way he enjoyed the attention being a cracker, albeit an old one not on a horse with a whip to crack and a pistol to fire, but now, he was on an ATV and an old doubled barrel twelve gauge shot gun with number eight bird shot.

So one afternoon, on one side of the fence, Teddy and his companion were on the look-out. The elderly ranch-hand was on the other side patrolling the fence line on his ATV. There was also a diamond back rattlesnake just minding his own business, and they all came together at the same time and place.

The ranch-hand saw the snake and turned his vehicle to run over him. The snake slithered through the fence and the ATV ran through the fence stopping just before hitting the woman. Teddy pulled right out of his collar and attacked the tire of the obvious aggressor as it was rolling toward his lady.

The tail of the snake was pinned under the tire and he thrashed about and awkwardly struck at Teddy, missed, and then struck the tire breaking his fangs. The elderly ranch-hand came out of the ATV with his shotgun and would have shot the snake except that the elderly woman was trying to hit the snake with her cane. She hit the shotgun causing the shot to blow out the tire. This enabled the snake to pull away leaving his rattlers broken off. Teddy bit down on the broken tail end of the snake.

Off went the snake with Teddy pulling and shaking his tail end. The ranch-hand came and blew off the snake's head and Teddy never let go of the tail end. In fact, he dragged and shook it all the way back to the tire and left it there.

That is the actual story, but somehow it evolved into several versions, none of which mattered one wit to Teddy who had no fear of the tire or the snake. It was all in a morning's work.

The old cracker made a hatband out of the snake hide and pinned his rattlers on one side of the hat. If anyone complemented his hat, he'd always tell the old back woods joke about "how the snake had six rattlers". He would usually pause and ponder as he spoke. And if the listener was familiar with snake lore, he would ask, "And a button?" And the cracker would laugh and say, "No, an asshole!"

TWO CATS

Once upon a time there was a man who would not marry a woman because she had five cats. Everyday, he would arrive at her place after work. Together, they sat around while she watched the news, had her cocktails, and played with the cats. Then it was to bed. He would always leave early in the morning to avoid the cats and go to his place. There he would dress, micro-wave a potpie, and then leave for work.

His name was Fred. Her name was Doris. She wanted to marry, but Fred said, "Too many cats!" One was enough. Well, it was not really the cats, but anything that may interfere with his life.

Interference to him was either animate or inanimate. For instance, a clock ticking or not ticking was an agitation to his psyche that sought solitude. He used clocks only to arrive on time at work, take breaks, and leave. Other than that he had no interest in clocks whatsoever, regardless if they were sundials, antiques, hour glasses, or atomic.

He was a file clerk with the county courthouse records department. He was good at his job, especially being accurate, punctual, and neat. Doris was a personal consular for a large company. She was good at her job too. She knew how to deal with people. She listened and applied common sense psychology. Psychology was her college degree; however, she considered most of the things that dealt with the id, ego, and subconscious not to be relevant to real life. To her Freud was a fake. Real life was current events, the news, the U.N., her cats, and how to cope.

Fred was just right for her. He didn't snore. He was a good lover, never asked for a meal, and did not want children. This was good because she didn't cook, do crafts, or decorate. She ate at the company cafeteria and had takeouts of "kitty pouches," not the crass "doggie bags". Her creativity was channeled only to her cats.

Fred would come to her place because the cats could not be left alone. Doris had two bedroomsone for her and one for the cats. Fred's place had only one bedroom. So the routine was setFred stayed at her place, while she listened to the news, had cocktails, played with the cats, and then they went to bed. She would make him a whiskey sour, which he sipped as he sat on the couch and waited for bedtime.

One of the cats was named Freud because he sat around and contemplated what Doris said was the meaning of cat dreams. Fred and Freud were comfortable in their apparent serenity. Freud liked to make the first move. He usually jumped up on the sofa and rubbed his chin against Fred's hand.

Cats have "I'm your friend" scent glands in their chinscalled pheromones. Without thinking, Fred rubbed Freud's ears. The pattern became habituala whiskey sour, a chin rub, ear and back stroking, and ignore the news as well as the other cats. There was no purring and especially no talking.

"Hey, Doris! Does Freud always sit around?"

"Oh yes. Since he was a little thing he has been a stuffed toy. Sometimes he breathes funny. Not funny ha-ha! Getting a little fat."

"Have you taken him to a vet?"

"No. None of my cats have ever been sick. All inside. Great kids. Adopted from the animal shelter. Had their first shots and fixing there. Nothing since. "

Fred stopped by the pet shop and bought some cat toys. Freud ignored them. They both sat. Fred had the feeling that Freud was trying to tell him something. On his day off Fred came by with a cat carrier and took Freud to the vet for a check up.

"Give him the works, Doc. He's my buddy. I'll come back later." The news was bad. Freud had a heart condition called dilated cardiomyopathy. It is a fatal disease. Fred treated as prescribed and developed an ache in his heart as Freud worsened. Freud died in Fred's lap.

Fred stayed at his place for a few days, and then a few weeks. Doris called daily and grief counseled over the phone. Then one day in the courthouse parking lot was a pick up truck with a sign "**Free To A Good Home**" painted on cardboard stuck on the tailgate. Fred leaned over and watched as two kittens tumbled and rolled about. Then his hand dropped down and the kittens ran over and chin rubbed his hand.

Fred took the kittens to his place for a nice meal. He gave them medical care at the vets and toys from the pet shop. Finally the grief from Freud's death was replaced by his love for the kittens.

Fred arrived unannounced at Doris's place with two kittens, a heart shaped box of chocolates and an engagement ring. He handed her a valentine card with a note: *Will you marry me? What are two more?*

He named the two new cats "Sig" and "Mund."

GAL AND GUY

A migratory family of the Great Depression settled on the north end of old Tampa Bay. They camped in a makeshift lean-to. Times were hard. They survived by fishing. Their great grand son, Samuel, now lives on their homestead and still fishes for a living.

His house is a "cracker house" that people would slow down to look at as they drove by. It should have become a historical site. The inside is a wood joiners dream. The warmth and peace that was felt upon entering was enhanced by the carpentry of all local woods in a harmonic blending of wood grains, colors, and fine joinery.

Outside was an open cypress bin, 4 X 12 X 4, with a prop-up lid. Assorted junk was scattered about, but the neighbors did not complain because Samuel was their source of oysters. The bin was used to hold oysters for "flushing".

Samuel would pole out to oyster beds and fill his skiff with a trip load of oysters. Then they went into the bin and turned on the pump. Pipes would spray the water to aerate and the overflow would end up on the ground. Corn meal hog food was then added. He sold the cleanest, fattest oysters anywhere. He refused to sell his oysters to restaurants. All sales were either cash or barter. In season he would catch or strike mullet and smoke them with a secret recipe. I was his part time vet that he bartered with for stray cat rabies shots. The smoked mullet, I believe, had some brown sugar added.

He worked off and on, in the **Super-Cabinet** shop; he was known for his quality workmanship. The owner pleaded with him to be a supervisor and train his workers, but he was chronically absent to fish, then constantly fired and rehired again.

One day he came into the animal hospital with two puppies he had taken in trade. Their names were Gal and Guy. The puppies were great. They were healthy, happy, and puppy curious. He allowed that he was monetarily short, so I traded the exams, worming, and vaccination for a burlap sack of oysters.

He informed me he was getting out of the fishing business as the times were changing. He said that his skiff was the last one that he would build. I knew the motor-well was in the middle, so the boat was of no use for recreational purposes. Of course I had heard the "I'm going to stop fishing" story before.

Samuel soon found another source of income. He would travel to a private dock on the bay in west Tampa and pick up a bag of cocaine. He placed it into a life jacket. He would make a run across the bay along Courtney Campbell causeway to Dog Beach in Pinellas County. A certain county commissioner had a recreational coke habit. He would be waiting under the Australian pines with two cheeseburgers. The skiff stopped in knee-deep water.

Samuel would put the life jacket on Gal. Gal and Guy would jump into the water and swim to get the burgers. The life jacket with the coke was removed, as Gal and Guy wolfed down the hamburgers, and replaced with another life jacket with the cash. The dogs would go back to the boat. Samuel helped them in and off they would go back to the private dock to exchange the money. Samuel got his cut. It was a real neat operation.

Recreational coke parties continued and resulted in a snitch. The police followed the trail and were waiting under the pines. The boat left the dock. Now Gal was in heat. Guy had mounted her a few times in the boat, but Samuel always batted him away with a paddle. When they got to the beach, Gal jumped into the water and Guy followed. They swam and their paws touched the bottom. This was the opportunity that Guy had been waiting for. He mounted Gal.

The commissioner ran out to get his buy. He was carrying the life jacket in one hand and the bag of burgers in his teeth. He threw the money jacket into the boat and started to take the one off of Gal. Guy's dog language insinuated, "don't mess with my baby!" Guy attacked the jacket and ripped it and the plastic bag open. Out spilled the coke.

What a scene! Samuel was yelling, the commissioner grappling, the cops charging, the coke dissolving, and the dogs? Well, doing what comes naturally.

A few days later my receptionist said, "Doc, Samuel wants a few words with you. He's leaving Gal to be spayed. She's been miss-mated."

Samuel was in a **Super-Cabinet** work uniform with *Samuel, Supervisor* inscribed on his shirt. He shook my hand and said, "I was fixing to quit anyways. The laws got no evidence, and I don't want no bastarderized-up puppies! I reckon it took a natural act to un-naturalize a few things."

I had no idea at the time what he was talking about, until another snitch (the secretary of the cabinet shop) came in with her cat. She told me the story... well, sort of.

The surgery went well.

TIPPY

Tippy was an obese, middle-aged, frustrated cat that viewed the world as his enemy, and furthermore, the enemy was always ready to attack especially when putting on an act of friendliness. He felt that it was better to strike first. So he thought and so he did. As his pupils dilated from fear, he struck.

The only decision he needed to make was the selection of the bite. He had three bites: a nip with incisors, a plunge with long teeth, and a tear that was a plunge with a twist of his head. Buried in his memory was the mind of the saber-toothed cat hunting around the tar pits.

Tippy watched all the time for an attack from the enemy and even faked his own naps. The enemy might have decided to use kindness as in warfare propaganda in order to trick him and then lull him into being caught off-guard. Yet Tippy was always on guard, vigilant, and ready to strike first.

He never apologized or said that he was sorry. Over time, his paranoia increased. He ate more and played less until he was medically obese. Then he started to hide. By his 8th birthday he was fearful of his birthday presents, particularly the gray stuffed toy mouse. There was no doubt that this mouse contained an evil spirit lurking underneath its fake skin.

He would sit and worry about, well, everything. Then he started to pull his hair out and lick his skin as a release of frustration. His rasp cat-tongue licked the hair off his body, skin included, and the appearance of Tippy displayed spots of baldness - very bald, as bald as a ping-pong ball.

Since he could not lick in certain areas, the hair loss developed into a balanced symmetrical appearance. Nonetheless, no sores had developed on these bald spots. Indeed, they were smooth and glabrous as a baby's behind. The owner did not like the hair-no-hair couture and considered it to be a skin disease. After many treatments with shampoos and lotions, the owner dropped Tippy off for an evaluation.

Tests revealed normal hair follicles and normal hair roots, but each hair was neatly cropped. Anti-anxiety tablets were dispensed. The licking stopped and the hair grew out. Now, there was plush hair on Tippy, the sofa, the bed, the carpet, etc. However, I was aware that it would take constant anesthesia to totally stop his misbehavior because I knew that it was something more, a deep-seated anxiety.

My theory proved to be correct as I received a note from the owner. It read:

Thank you for taking such good care of Tippy. He will take his pill in a strawberry Fig Newton. His hair coat is beautiful. And he seems to be more of his old self again. He bit me several times today to punish me. Thanks again.

PROZAC THE FID

Prozac was a long tailed macaw. He was given to Jason by his mother in hopes that Jason would care for him and come out of his shell. Jason was an early teenager who was on Prozac for his anxieties. Why not replace Prozac with Prozac?

Prozac was not as bird-brained as people who do not know birds tend to think. Parrots are intelligent, have the ability to reason, and also have feelings. Plus, he was beautiful. He had a magnificent tail and yellow-ringed eyes. His toes were two in front and two behind. He usually grabbed the rail with one foot, balanced, and held a Brazil nut in his left foot. Then, he would crack the nut with his powerful beak. He was left-footed in the same manner that humans are left-handed.

Time passed. Jason cleaned Prozac's cage and changed his food and water. He started talking to Prozac, but Prozac remained mute, and he wondered why this person was repeatedly saying, "You are so pretty."

Prozac contemplated, "Of course I am pretty. Bring me more nuts! Preening is okay, but I'd like to get outside. Get jess straps if you worry about me flying away!"

Jason searched the web and found information about macaws. The parrot family fascinated him—then it was other birds. He became a bird watcher. A local group of birders welcomed him. He joined, but his interest developed more into the biology of birds. He took a feather to the biology lab at school and marveled at the anatomy and physics of flight. He talked his mother into buying a whole frozen turkey. It was not even close to being Thanksgiving.

Jason dissected and identified the bones and muscles. He even learned the Latin and Latinized Greek names of all the organs, bones, muscles, and nerves of the bird. Jason, now sans pills, became an ace at biology. He studied avian parasitology, hematology, and other –ologies. He was invited to lecture in high school classes.

At home Jason would sit by Prozac and study. Between chapters he would say, "You are so pretty," without looking up. Prozac did not respond.

Spring was time to have Prozac's wings clipped in order to finally take him outside. They went by increments, starting from the porch, moving to the yard, and then the park. Jason would sit and read with Prozac on his shoulder enjoying all of their surroundings. Between chapters Jason still said, "You are so pretty," but Prozac still didn't respond. Not a word. Jason received an honors scholarship in biology at the university. He came home after mid-term exams. Prozac did not greet him. Prozac felt orphaned.

Instead, Prozac thought, "Let's go to the park. Where have you been? Books… books! There is more to life!"

Jason took a book and with Prozac on his shoulder, went to the park, and sat on a bench. A young lady admired the bird. Prozac cocked his head and said, "You are so pretty!"

They both laughed. She sat down and they discovered that they both went to the same college. Every day they met in the park. Then it became lunch at the park and feeding Prozac nuts. Jason took Prozac to college with him, and the young lady made the twosome a threesome after courtship.

Prozac became their FID—*Feathered KID*—and he would greet her with, "You are so pretty!"

LANCELOT'S CASTLES

A standard white poodle named Lancelot had castles. He was not house broken and the maid placed small plastic buckets upside down over his poop. Later, the maid scooped his poop into his buckets forming castles (like children making sand castles on the beach), pressed the lid tight, and took Lancelot's castles to the garbage. In spite of the castles, the house smelled of poop.

Man—Marty, woman—Helen, and canine—Lancelot, all lived in a quasi relationship. Lancelot was in the category of a Beta fish in a tank that was benignly cared for.

He was fed and watered. Monthly, a professional groomer would come by in a van. Lancelot was bathed, clipped, and brushed. The groomer would also pluck his ears and give him a pedicure. Yearly, a mobile vet would visit in order to examine, vaccinate, and test his blood, feces, and urine.

Usually nothing else was happening so that his attention could be focused on his castles. He pooped small amounts scattered about and watched as his poop was covered with a castle. Viewed from the ceiling, the castles were placed so as —to form patterns. Lancelot's favorite was the diamond pattern. The carpet in the living area was by far the best place for the diamond pattern. A diamond pattern on that carpet was *ce'st magnifique*—he was a French poodle. He had poop carte blanche except the bedroom.

The bedroom was where Marty and Helen stayed. On the weekends, Marty and Helen rotated between three hotels. They were active members of a party group called **PDPU**—Party Down Party Up. Their life was work, out to eat, TV in bed, and weekends with

PDPU. Lancelot was alone. Making castles was his only life. For all three it was a lonely anemic life, until Princess—the girl next door. She was a light-cream yellow Labrador Retriever. As she came into heat, Lancelot forgot about his castle formations. He would dig under the fence, and Princess accepted him as her mate. Although the neighbors complained, it was decided to let Princess have the puppies.

Early one morning Marty and Helen were called over to witness the delivery of six puppies. Lancelot was included. He behaved as a father should at the birthing—proud, attentive, and out of the way.

The puppies were adorable. They were called *Poolabs*. The *Poolabs* opened their eyes, were weaned, and both couples marveled at their puppy hood. Princess let everyone join in on the marvel of puppy hood. It fascinated them as they all felt part of the miracle. Carefully selected homes were found for the puppies. Princess was spayed, and Marty and Helen had skipped five **PDPU** meetings.

As they took Lancelot for walks, Princess often came along. They waved to neighbors. Again, it was time for another **PDPU** gathering. By mutual looks and feelings, they decided to drop out and have a baby instead. They had discovered each other.

Lancelot changed his lifestyle. He pooped outside, always in one corner. No more castles were needed. The carpets were replaced for the baby on the way. And of course they all lived happily thereafter. They had discovered life and found mutual love. They would usually joke and say it was "puppy love".

All had found Camelot.

SWISSY FROM SWITZERLAND

Once upon a time a young woman went to a place called Switzerland where they make great chocolate. Her name was Bernice and she had been adopted as a baby girl by a wealthy couple. She was beyond spoiled-rotten and by the time of her teen-age years she still considered that the world revolved around her personal self.

After graduating from a private high school, she wished to go to Switzerland to study art, snow ski, and loose her virginity to a handsome ski instructor with long eyelashes, an accent, good abs, and sexual experience. After all, the rich awkward acne boys in her private school were - well, like you know - dumb.

And so she went. Within two weeks she had a live-in lover who - well, like you know - was marvelous. It was a marginal pseudo-marriage of sorts. The French use the word *gigolo* for such an arrangement. Anthropologists consider it to be based upon "Sex For Meat" and feminists describe it as denigration. Biologists thought of it as a symbiotic relationship in which both organisms live in a closely with mutual benefits. One individual does not benefit solely such as in parasitism.

A good analogy for such a high-quality mutual relationship is microbial flora in ruminates. Bacteria in the digestive tract of ruminants (cows and other cud chewers) are furnished food, and in the process of utilizing the food they produce nutrients for the "host" - both benefit.

Swissy was a puppy of questionable ancestry in a pet shop window in Bern. Bernice had to have him and of course the pet shop took her Platinum Master Card. Over time her self-centered, narcissist psyche, transferred to Swissy. He was called Swissy because he was a Swiss dog, and anything else would have been - well, like you know - dumb. Swissy was spoiled and accepted his role as her consoler. He let her hold him and carry him around, talking to him, kissing him, and hugging him.

She started to skip art classes to be with Swissy and her sexual partner, for he had awakened her to the pleasure of sex. His expertise had trained her to all the nuances, techniques, and positions of sex. She was an eager learner, but had one flaw. She kept both Swissy and her lover with her in bed. All three symbiosed until Swissy became a teenager.

As Swissy became a teenager, his testosterone began to rise. It had risen so much that one time during sex, Swissy mounted Bernice's belly and began to hump her navel. Swissy enjoyed it so much that it became what Bernice called, "Well, like you know, something we should *all* enjoy."

The ski instructor with the long eyelashes was amused at first, and then he became puzzled. He thought, "Kinky," until finally he got ticked off. Most people would agree.

He had learned his sexual art after his long experiences with the rejected, the misfits, the psychotics, the Jewish American Princesses, the bored, and the *whatever*, but this experience was close to being borderline insanity. He thought, "What was she? Perhaps she was a throw back to ancient fertility rites. Perhaps she was reincarnated Ashtorteh? Would she engage in bestiality? Was this relationship worth saving?"

Then he decided that it was Swissy, and the solution was that Swissy needed to be fixed, i.e., made a eunuch, put in neutral. He was a miniature metzgerhund - butcher dog. Swissy was superfluous to his relationship with Bernice.

When Bernice went to her weekly class in Renaissance Art History, he kidnapped Swissy and took him to his uncle's veterinary clinic. It was explained that he had a new pet that he wanted to be neutered. The question was, "Could some sort of testicular implant make him still appear as if he had not been neutered?"

After all, his vocation was recreational sex education. He hated the French word *gigolo*, and a vacuous limp scrotum for such a calling was, well, as Bernice would say, "Like, you know - dumb."

Bernice was distraught over the lost Swissy. She blamed her lover for letting him run away. She stopped his allowance and ended her affair and threw him out. She advertised, posted up photographs with a reward: $$$$$, and she went daily to the animal shelter.

Meanwhile back at the animal hospital Swissy was held under a pseudonym, neutered, and kept until the scar healed. He was also given a shot of progesteronea hormone of pregnancy. Not only was he now a eunuch, but also he thought he was pregnant. Plus, the vet implanted silicone shaped testicles so that Swissy looked normal.

The vet had no ethical problems with this operation since Swissy was not of show dog stature. Also he knew that his nephew was a sexual addict and often called him "Pudenda Pete" when his real name, Peter, was apt enough.

During Swissy's transformation, another transformation was taking place. Bernice started volunteering for the animal shelter and her narcissism waned as compassion for the homeless, the abused, and the infirm animals entered her soul. She became simon-pure.

When it was time, Swissy appeared at the animal shelter as a found stray and Bernice rejoiced. Peter hoped for a reconciliation, which did not happen. He moved on. Bernice and Swissy promptly went back to Connecticut and lived happily ever after. The reason for the "happily ever after" is because as a volunteer at the local animal shelter, Bernice met and married one of the board members who was older and wealthy in real estate.

All three - well, like you know - enjoyed. Swissy contently stayed in his own private room with a cashmere blanket, multiple toys, and light classical background music.

The Swiss experience had saved Bernice's psyche. Her erstwhile Swiss lover restricted his lovers to neighboring countries, especially German women. He claimed they were almost his equal in bed and above all no-nonsense.

I had a Swiss Army Knife as a boy scout and I know the Swiss make great multipurpose tools. They also make good watches, great chocolate, and are renowned bankers. Now I am aware that they are probably the first to have made doggie implant testicles.

A veterinarian from Switzerland at a convention in Orlando, Florida, told me most of the above story over breakfast. He said that he had used silicone from the hardware store to mold the testicles. I suppose it is true - of course they do like to yodel a lot, and like you know, I added a few extra details.

HER ROYAL HIGHNESS'S BUSINESS

Ms. Mooney walked Mildred in the early morning to do her business. Mildred was a Shih Tzu with hair to her feet and a ribbon in a topknot. Her coat was regal. Indeed, she was treated as a royal person, and of course, Ms. Mooney addressed using the royal, "we". There was a lot of other minor royal stuff, too. For instance, her topknot ribbons were purple and gold. She even drank French bottled water.

Ms. Mooney was divorced from a very controlling partner and Mildred was her only child. Not really, for Mildred was not child like; however, she enjoyed being spoiled, and she returned love in full measure.

"It's time for your royal highness's morning business. You are such a cutie pie. My little sweetums. Snap the leash and off we go."

Ms. Mooney walked Mildred for her "royal business" early in the morning because she worked at the hospital as a doctor's assistant. Mildred's business was quickly picked up with the morning newspaper's plastic bag. Mildred's butt was gently cleaned with a baby wipe that went into the bag and with a knot, it was all tied so neatly together. "Royal business done."

A male neighbor woke early one morning. He was picking up the newspaper when Ms. Mooney stopped for Mildred to do her business. Mildred obliged and the clean up was done quickly, and oh, so neat!

"Blustering Mike!" The man said, "No dog poops in my yard!"

"Baloney! It's the road's right of way! Besides, it's all picked up!"

"Baloney Double Bee! Dog poop is full of germs and worms! Get on the road!"

"Get out of the way! It's public property! Why don't you go back in and read the paper? Try acting your age."

"Why don't you slop mop here and get on the road."

"If you wish to stand on public property blocking our way, go right ahead. We will walk around you onto your property, ta-ta!"

In the past, Mike the neighbor had seemed nice enough. He had helped her start the car when there was a poor battery connection. She thought he might be acceptable as a companion after her controlling husband. She had vowed to never be a victim again. Now, Mike was trying to control not only her, but Mildred too. That insulted her royalty.

The easy way out was to walk on the other side of the road, and she almost did, but on her day off, she went to the city department of roads and checked out the right of way. She was advised that it was public property and as long as she cleaned up, it was okay. She was satisfied, but Mike was not. The confrontation escalated.

"Well, little precious, we will just have to see who controls what. Is it public? Is it our personal business? That's it! It is our business! We go together. I'll snap the leash. There little miss cuteness, your royal highness, we have to fight back. You know when we're right, we are right."

"When you are right, you are right." Thought Ms. Mooney as Mildred sniffed, pawed the grass, circled, and finally squatted. Upon this day when she squatted, Ms. Mooney raised the bar. She hiked her robe and squatted in mime. Then she cleaned up, wiped Mildred's butt and proceeded. The royal business was briskly over.

Next day, Mike took a photograph of them squatting and took it to court. The judge was shown a 8 X 10 blow up, in color, of the two squatters. The defense was - a: no nudity, b: Ms. Mooney was simply "observing" a proper poop from her little dog, c: Mrs. Mooney would never publicly urinate, and d: Mrs. Mooney sang in the Lutheran church choir. And since, she was a doctor' assistant, she had devoted her life to the care of the sick and infirm. The judge threw the case out. There was a reporter at the hearing who thought this was one of those "human interest" stories. The editor gave it the front page of the Metro Section.

The next day, there was a small group of people on the right of way with a local TV station, recording. They would all lift up their raincoats and squat on command. A twelve year old opened a lemonade stand. It was fun. After a few days, it was over.

Mike mellowed and even laughed and bought some lemonade for Ms. Mooney and commented that they were all "M's", and that possibly three "M's" could get along.

"Hey, it's Mooney, Mike and Mildred. What kind of mutt is it?" He asked.

"It's a she, and she is a Shih Tzu."

"She's a "shit zoo" for sure! How about some coffee? I bought a doggie treat?"

KACHINA DOLLS

Robert and Rachel called each other by name with precise, clipped, or even truncated endingsin the same manner used by a parent who calls to their child caught with their hand in the cookie jar. They usually introduced themselves as, "Old R & R," not for "Robert and Rachel," but for "Rocking and Rolling," and indeed they were R&R-ing right along into their early seventies. They spent three months of each year R&R-ing in their mobile RV, touring various parts of the USA. By early May, they were on the road again and back in Oldsmar by Labor Day.

Two Siamese cats went with them. Any one of the four would be insulted not to go along. I always checked over Si and Am before and after each trip, "just to be safe," Robert and Rachel jointly said one time. This time, Si had some conjunctivitis that required a swab for cytology and eye drops. Am checked out O.K.

During the examination, Robert and Rachel bantered back and forth, not as a *tête-à-tête*, but more open to be heard by my office staff. Their conversation was as breezy as they were.

"We will have to buy a present for our ***Toys For Tots*** donation this year because all of the dolls stay with us."

Then, Robert said, "It was not my idea to buy the first doll."

"You know that one doll is not going to satisfy both cats."

"Rachel, one doll was good enough for a Hopi dancer. I liked the Mud Head."

"Si liked the Mud Head, and Am glared at her. I knew it! Just knew it! Jealously among siblings! There is jealously between them, you know."

"We did not have to buy another doll. They were content. They took turns."

"No! Robert, it was simply a case of sibling rivalry. We needed another doll."

"Rachel, the second doll started the whole thing. How many Kachina dolls are there left in Arizona?"

"Listen, you buy one, and then you have to buy two, and so forth. You, of course, realize that they caught on right away as to the sacred implications of the dolls."

"At our age, we do not need sacred fertility dances or rain dances. Our sprinkler system works just fine. And as to our fertility systems, forget it!"

"There is a connection to all our ancestors through the dolls. You would know that if you ever read the horoscopes or noticed that story about the mummified cats."

"My dear, the Egyptian cat mummies are not Hopi. Wrong continent!"

"Si wanted one. Then Am had to have one, and then Si. You see? Simple!"

"No I don't see. I had to keep calling back to the shop to have the dolls expressed to our next stop. We are going to give at least four of the dolls to **Toys For Tots**."

"We keep the dolls and buy a toy stove to give. It is really all your fault, you know. You wanted to go to Arizona! You were the one that voted for that horrible Goldwater!"

"Now Rachel, leave Goldwater out. That was years ago. You are begging the question. We have a small fortune in Kachina dolls. At least give two away!"

By now, I was through with the exams. They left still continuing with the back and forth banter, better known as - *chitchat*. They left the eye medication on the counter and I took it out to the RV, a thirty-four foot Pathfinder. I knocked.

"Do come in," said Robert, "If you can get in."

There were Kachina dolls everywhere. There was a tunnel for the cats through a pile of dolls. It was a Kachina doll Siamese cat warren. Rachel was playing patty-cake with Si while Am sulked.

She nodded to me and said, "Thanks so much, Dr. Robert. Goldwater did lose. Get over it."

"It was that damn commercial. The one with the little girl in the field picking daisies and . . ."

"I am so sick of hearing about that commercial. Look at Am! He is jealous! Come here baby. Your turn for patty."

What a wonderful thing is the human-animal bond; a heart to love, a face to kiss, a joy to watch. All of these moments lift me in times of depression over the neglected ones and the dying ones. How much love and joy they give us, asking so little in return, except a Kachina doll or two, or four, or . . .

THE STUDLY

Often there is a psychological refusal by the human male to neuter non-human males. A male cat named Studly fell into that category. He was turned out at night to fulfill his name and his namesake.

Studly was Mister's cat. Mister, the owner, nicknamed himself Mr. Studly after his cat. Mr. Studly had taken in a female roommate and they had a conditional arrangement to see if Mr. Studly and Miss were compatible enough for a future Mr. and Mrs. Studly commitment.

Studly, by his own choice, slept in the garage on a shelf that had a neat little cat condo unit with **THE STUDLY** raised in red plastic lettering across the top like a storefront sign. Studly napped, groomed, and nibbled during the day. At night he was out "tomcatting." Each household member knew their turf and so a relationship was able to develop.

Studly came very close to being neutered, stemming from a bite received by a rival male cat in a territorial fight. The bite was deep and abscessed. The wound was near the scrotum and required surgical debridement—removal of all diseased tissues—and a Z-plasty type of sliding viable skin to cover the large open wound. The future Mrs. had rolled her eyes, sighed, and left firm directions that by no means were we to castrate Studly. It would have been much easier to castrate Studly and use the scrotal tissue to cover the wound, but we followed the given directions and the wound healed nicely.

Mr. and Mrs. Studly married. They made reservations for a dream two-week stay at the Anhinga Resort, which had a nature walk, workout room, tennis court, and a pool large enough for laps. A pre-teen neighbor agreed to come in after school for ten dollars and change the food and water and leave the garage door cracked open with a cinder block. The car was packed and the trip could be made in one day if they choose to leave early enough in the morning, which they did. That night they left the garage door blocked and opened over night, and by chance the passenger sidecar window down.

Since the car was filled with new stuff from the wedding gifts, it was natural enough for Studly to mark it as part of his territory. He selected the front seats, and of course cats mark with urine. Cat urine has tiny droplets of fat suspended in it and the droplets absorb testosterone, which gives a unique odor to the urine that is repulsive to humans. In fact the vapor is a form of biological torture that produces nausea, headaches, and impotency in humans as reported in the *Minnesota Urology and Pithecoid Journal of Medicine*.

Studly went overboard in that he squeezed every drop of urine he had, rested for two hours, and then pushed out some more. Before daylight, Mr. and Mrs. took off for a vacation to celebrate their new marriage. As they drove, only one block away, they did an immediate U-turn. They used every spray in the house to little avail. They drove with windows down and stopped three miles later and purchased cans of sprays including: insecticides, deodorizers and room fresheners—nothing helped.

At the next stop they tried furniture polish, antibacterial spray, and body deodorant—still nothing helped. Finally, they fell in-line behind a semi belching burnt diesel fuel that somewhat masked the odor. Their next stop was *Meg's Dog and Cat Grooming Shop*. They purchased animal odor neutralizers, both sprays and shampoos. Not much help there either.

When they arrived at the resort they never used their car, for it was left to air out. All in all, with two weeks of airing out, they were able to drive their marked   car, with open windows, back home.

Mr. Studly came into the office with Studly requesting a neuter for "The Studly" and laughing added, "Not for me! I'm married now."

DANIEL WEBSTER

Not so long ago there was an eight-pound mixed terrier dog that answered the phone, door chimes, and other noises. He had been trained to be a deaf dog at Angell Memorial Animal Hospital in Boston. The owner was Mrs. Webster, who was partially deaf from an accidental explosion that damaged her middle and internal ears. She thought that the little dog was quite an orator, so she named him Daniel, and addressed him as, "The Senator Daniel Webster."

She lived alone. Her husband of thirty odd years had died, and their two children had moved out of state. They never called, wrote, or visited. They were the upwardly mobile types who considered Mom to be old fashioned. What they didn't know was that she had a lot of old fashioned money. She felt and was abandoned until Daniel came into her life, and the two bonded with great love and respect.

Daniel would run to her with a high pitch—*yip, yip, yip, yip, yip*. Then he would pause and signal the door with four more yips—*yip, yip, yip, yip*; the phone with two yips—*yip, yip*; or some unknown with one yip—*yip*. If the unknown sound came from the window he would yip all the way to the window. He yipped for everything. He would run to Mrs. Webster with a yip, yipping the whole way, and then still with a yip, yip to the phone.

Mrs. Webster was a sixth generation Bostonian; besides, Massachusetts was the center of the world. Her old neighborhood had degenerated somewhat over time. She had many antique treasures and a 1943 copper penny. Her will was to leave it all to the Angell Memorial Animal Hospital in trust to care for Daniel, and when he died they could keep the rest.

She was one to rarely visit the outside. Her groceries, medicines and sundries were delivered. Television and Daniel entertained her world. She watched the soaps, the news, and public broadcasting. Nourishment was frozen microwave and green tea with cream and sugar. Daniel had canned food and a little cream on top. She lounged in a sweat suit, bedroom shoes, and a shawl most of the day. She trained Daniel to use a towel spread on the closet floor. Every three or four days she would roll it up and throw it away. She kept everything nice and neat. When she did go out, she dressed as a proper lady, not as an old *dowager*. She rode in cabs and gave generous tips. The cabbies knew her by name and enjoyed opening doors for her, but she always would call a neighbor and give them the route and estimated time of arrival back home, for safety.

The grocery delivery person was a new one. He took her groceries into the kitchen and unpacked them on the kitchen table. He introduced himself as Evans, and told her the story about how he got his name. His high-school baseball coach—he grew up near Fenway Park—had called him by his surname and not his given name. Evans it was and it stuck. Baseball was really not his thing. He was working two jobs and had finished one year in Boston College. Now he had worked enough to finish another semester. He did not want to borrow money. He thought that he would borrow later for a house or something.

Daniel sniffed and checked him out. He passed. None of the others had even come close to passing, but Evans was accepted. When he delivered to the neighborhood, he would often drop by for short visits. Four crisp knocks on the door and Daniel would answer with four sharp yips. Daniel would jump in Evans' lap. All three engaged in a little playtime and some chitchat, mostly about Mrs. Webster's life, antiques, and the latest current events.

One day there was four crisp knocks, four sharp yips, but the door stayed locked. Evans returned the next day, knocked, and heard the yips, but no Mrs. Webster. He inquired with the neighbors, and then called the police. Mrs. Webster was slumped in her rocking chair. She was dead. The police said it was natural causes and the medical examiner wrote cardiac failure. An envelope was discovered on the marble topped Victorian bedside table with EVANS written on it. It also contained an attorney's name.

Evans was to stay in the house and care for Daniel. The trust paid for his education and living expenses. Daniel now got to walk in the park and the two were companions. Because of Daniel, Evans shifted his major to chemistry and two years later was accepted into the Veterinary College at Tufts. Daniel did not accept most of Evans' lady friends, even though some spent the night. Some of Evans' friends referred to the place as The Addams' House, due to the décor. Daniel remained aloof.

Then, Donna, a woman from the same freshman class in vet school entered into Evan's life. She was accepted. During his last year in college, Daniel developed lymphoma. After only four months of therapy, it was finally time. They had been together for six years, four of the six years with Donna. The grief for Daniel was as intense as it was for Mrs. Webster's departure, but Daniel had chosen well. Evans and Donna were married the day after graduation.

Their first child was named Daniel Webster Evans.

FAITH AND CALVIN

Hap was the head custodian of a Presbyterian church. He was in charge of the church, the grounds, the out-buildings, and the minister's house—which is called a *manse*. The property extended for 40 acres and included a soccer field. He had an office in the maintenance building, a permanent crew of four, and never lacked a volunteer. There was always someone who would donate time or money for a project.

On occasion, there would be different opinions--such as the color of paint or what kind of landscaping plant to use. The board of deacons did the day-to-day overseeing of all tactical operations. The elders along with the pastor created the strategy. The church, as are all Presbyterian churches, was well organized—its ministers educated, and the members dedicated. The church library kept a *Geneva Bible* to insure the accuracy of the *King James Bible*.

Hap's family was part of the congregation. It became a custom that they received first-refusal on used things that needed replacing. Most items were sold in a semi-annual yard sale. The church flourished.

It was built in 1866 out from Columbus, Ohio, by a family that had seen four of their sons go to the Civil War. They donated forty acres of their one hundred sixty acre homestead that was given to them by the Homestead Act of 1862, championed by President Lincoln. All of their sons had returned. Only two were wounded. It was their thanks to God.

The church was rebuilt or added onto in 1880, 1900, and there after to retain the tradition every twenty years. Each time it was enlarged and more amenities were added. It evolved from the strict fundamental Calvinistic congregation to becoming more secular at the chagrin of a few holdouts. For instance, it was now okay to go shopping on Sunday, which used to be reserved from the Sabbath— a day of rest and prayer. Members could dance, play cards, and do many other things that had previously been sinful. Also, now the once rural church was suburban and had an enviable forty acres.

It advertised in the phone book yellow pages and included a nursery, preschool, day care, youth group, singles group, women's group, men's group, couples group, music group, a bookstore, soccer field, and even a web site. It was all for the good of the members. But there was one exception.

His name was Joel and he was the oldest elder, arthritic and wheezy, but had a mind as he said, "like a steel trap." He voted against what he called the Devil's work. He carried a copy of the orange *Westminster Shorter Catechism* in his shirt pocket and quoted it by page and line from memory. He could quote scriptures and the *Westminster Confession of Faith*.

In fact, he was a widower and very lonely.

At times, Joel made for difficult situations. But the elders kept Joel at bay long enough, which allowed him to forget all about the ruckus that he had caused. Eventually Joel converted and did what was "good for the members" rather than hassle over scripture.

Early one Sunday morning as Hap was making his rounds in the parking lot in his tractor and trailer, he found a cardboard box with two puppies asleep in a blanket. He decided to take them home to his family, but first he dutifully reported it to the board of deacons. The deacons were in the middle of an Easter Sunrise planning and referred the question to the elders.

"Not much to decide. Just give the puppies to the humane shelter," Joel intervened.

The puppies belonged to the congregation and that was that. To end the discussion it was decided to give the care of the puppies to Hap, the custodian. Joel could pick one puppy when they were older. Joel picked the male and named him Calvin. Hap named the female Faith.

Each day Joel came while Hap worked, and played with Calvin and brought him a ceramic bowl and a harness. They then went for a walk and left Faith behind. As the puppies grew, they did all of the things that puppies do, such as teething, playful aggression, and of course they gave open love and affection.

Puppyhood was over and Faith started into heat.

Joel came to pick up Calvin for his afternoon walk and found Calvin and Faith sexually united, fastened together in what breeders call a tie. Joel disapproved of people dancing. This was too much! And it was on church grounds! And it was all Faith's fault! And Faith was the ward of Hap; therefore Hap needed probation.

The elders had to listen and force themselves to look serious.

One suggested that Faith be spayed before the birthing.

Joel spoke and said, "The sixth commandment forbideth the taking away of our own life, or the life of a neighbor unjustly, or whatsoever tendth thereunto. "The puppies tendth thereunto. Hap was the ward of a harlot. "Deuteronomy 23:18, 'Thou shalt not bring the hire of a harlot, or the wages of a dog, into the house of Jehovah thy God for any vow: for both these are an abomination unto Jehovah thy God.'"

He slammed the table, "Dang it! Incest! On the Lord's land! Brother and sister! Gol dang it!" Joel sat down. He was embarrassed as "Gol dang" was harsh language for him.

He then stood up again, "There were no Easter eggs in Jerusalem, so there."

Easter planning was a pressing matter and it was quickly decided that Hap was to have general care of Faith and her puppies, but that Joel would now be in total charge of Calvin. Faith had three puppies that quickly found homes among the congregation. She was spayed and Joel started to come by early afternoons to take Calvin for walks. After a few weeks, Joel, Hap, Faith, and Calvin all went on the walks.

Joel brought Faith a ceramic bowl and a harness to match Calvin's.

They called themselves, "The Four Musketeers". Joel was no longer lonely. He cared for the dogs and had them vaccinated and "fixed", as he stated. A year passed and it was now Easter again. Hap and Joel dressed as Easter bunnies and Faith and Calvin had rabbit ears for the big Easter egg hunt.

There was peace between all. Joel mumbled, "It was all predestination anyway."

TORQUE

Betty bought an eight-week-old Rottweiler puppy named Torque. Until that day, Betty's life consisted of exercise, diet, clients, and an aloofness from social contacts. She jogged, meditated, and lived in harmony with her inner self and environs.

Betty, enjoying the way she was, decided that all of her attributes were also those of a Rottweiler, so she found a male puppy from a breeder advertisement.

The puppy pulled a chew toy from her hand with a steady twist of his head and neck muscles...no jerking, just a power twist. "His name has to be Torque!" There was instant bonding.

Torque grew into eighty-four pounds of show ring quality muscle. He exuded strength that was quietly controlled. Betty knew that he would die for her and she felt the same. She cleaned his eyes, ears, and lower lips daily, and bathed him once weekly in aloe and oatmeal shampoo. On their walks no one flirted with her and no one dared to even approach; however, a few nodded.

Lakeside Park had a set aside area for dogs and a six-mile trail around the wooded area. One afternoon while jogging along the trail, Torque's ears perked up and he slalomed to the grassy edge. A squad of bees that were scouting out a thrown away candy wrapper stung him. He was stoic and stings did not bother himhe had been stung before, but his face started to swell.

By the time Betty got him to the emergency vet his eyes were shut and he was having trouble breathing. His skin erupted into hives. The vet said that he was having an anaphylactic reaction that could be fatal if he went into shock. Emergency measures were necessary. Betty sat with him during the emergency treatment. He had an indwelling catheter, fluids, epinephrine, antihistamines, glucocorticoids, and oxygen. He recovered. The shock organ in dogs is the liver, and Torque showed no liver damage.

Their next trip was to the park. At the entrance, an armed sheriff stood tall. He advised, "Do not go into the park. We are looking for an armed and dangerous serial killer. Although, we have just swept the trail so it should be safe. This guy is a psycho, so please…Be careful."

Betty rubbed some insect repellant on Torque's head and on her cap bill. They jogged down the trail and just past a sharp turn, Torque froze. Like an English Pointer approaching a covey of quail, he slowly with fixed eyes approached a culvert. Torque's lips curled and a volcanic growl from a muscle tensed body rumbled as a warning. Betty fled.

Torque closed like a martial arts Tae Kwon Do expert . . . all of his senses concentrated into one. The killer had always been the dominant person who caused fear. Now he was fearful. The unshaven mud spattered killer was in a fetal position hiding in the culvert. As he came out of the culvert, he crouched and pointed his pistol at Torque.

Torque lunged. With his head, Torque pushed the pistol arm up as a shot went off. With his powerful neck and shoulder he pushed against the killer's chest hard enough to knock him down flat on his back. One paw swipe and the pistol was thrown into the bushes.

Torque mounted the killer. Bared teeth and a constant rumbling growl sent a clear message to the man. The killer knew that he was going to die. He was paralyzed with terror.

Two officers arrived with guns drawn.

The killer was cuffed as he yelled and cursed Torque "God

Almighty! That damn dog! He is crazy! Crazy! Crazy! A beast from hell!"

But not so the officers, "Good dog. Good boy. Good dog."

Just then a butterfly flitted near Torque's head. The residual memory of near death with the bees flooded Torque's psyche. He cowered and shook and backed away.

One officer said, "I don't believe it! This dog is a K-9 SWAT team who disarms and captures a 250-pound psycho killer. Look at him now! A butterfly spooks him. What an ending! Go figure."

MAFIA CAT

The Walton's children were grown and gone. They now had the empty nest syndrome. She was a homemaker, and he, a retired insurance adjuster. For thirty odd years he had put up with claims that he considered borderline fraudulent. Now he had no one to distrust.

Mr. Walton puttered about the house and yard. He disagreed with all the news reports and even cursed the insects. He moaned that the dishwasher manufactures had created poor designs. Why else was he unable to load it properly? He was responsible for some inside chores, the book-keeping, and watching soaps on TV, which was the only time when Mr. was not grumbling and he was able to take a daytime nap.

Mrs. Walton clipped coupons from the paper, read the obits, and did the crosswords. She saw an ad with a picture of a cat for adoption from the animal shelter. She went there and saw the many homeless and abandoned cats. She noticed one cat that was beautifully orange in color. He was backed into the corner of his kennel with his ears laid back. He hissed.

"What is wrong with this one?"

"He's going to be put down. History of biting people. Let me check his chart. That's right. Two more days of observation and he's going to be put to sleep. Have to keep biters for ten days of observation after they bite a person. Public health law."

"I'll take him."

"Not recommended. Sign a waiver. Come back after the weekend. I'll put a hold on his chart. Good Luck! He is cranky! Name is Pumpkin. I think he may be some kind of alien."

The new home, in a way, was helpful to Pumpkin. His disposition improved toward Mrs. Walton. But Mr. Walton was hissed and spat at and even clawed once. Mr. Walton hated Pumpkin. He kept saying that Pumpkin was an outlaw, a sociopath, a mental case, and that he was proof that a kitty hell existed because that was where Pumpkin was headed.

As time went on Pumpkin became a wedge in their marriage.

"You are so stubborn! Leave him alone! You would argue with a signpost and take the wrong road for spite! You're used to having your own way. Get used to the cat!"

"What kind of cat will not let you brush him? He has to be sedated and his hair clipped in that god-awful lion cut you think is so cute. The cat is mafia! He hates his own body. That is why he gets mats. Damn killer cat!"

It was a futile argument in that Mrs. Walton had found an outlet for her maternal instinct and solved her empty-nest syndrome. Pumpkin adopted her and considered Mr. Walton to be his enemy. One time when Pumpkin was at the vet for sedation and a lion-cut Mr. Walton put in a personal phone call to the veterinarian.

"Doc, Mr. Walton here! That Pumpkin cat from hell needs an overdose! My permission to overdose! OD-ed is the answer. End his misery! His life must be terrible. He hates everything and attacks anything that moves and he disagrees with all of the above. He pees on the sofa where I sit! Just do it!"

"I cannot do that. Let's try some tranquilizers. That might help. Then there are hormones, behavior counseling, and . . ."

"Doc, I'll make it worth your while. How does a hundred sound? Hey, he had a heart attack or something."

"His heart is fine. I can not help you."

"Man, man! How about two. Is there such a thing as a cat hit man? Thanks anyway. I'll think of something."

Tranquilizers were worthless. More like giving him a treat. Mr. and Mrs. Walton were watching a murder mystery on TV, and the victim was killed by an overdose of insulin.

"Hmmm …" Mr. Walton thought to himself, "That's a possibility. How could I get near the little fart? When he is sleeping? Where do I give the shot? How much? Naw … A baseball bat? … Gotta think of something."

Just then, Mrs. Walton announced great news. "Dear, I'm going to visit my mother for a week or so. She is not well. Tale care of Pumpkin. Clean his litter daily and fresh water and don't leave his food down for more than two hours."

"Now is my chance. Someway you are going to die! First you must suffer. Gulag!" thought Mr. Walton joyously.

Pumpkin wondered why his food bowl was neglected. On day one, Pumpkin stared curiously at Mr. Walton. On day two, he squinted his eyes over the empty food bowl. Day three, he ground his teeth. Day four, he hid.

"You little snot. Why don't you beg?"

Day eight, Mrs. Walton came home. She did not see Pumpkin. He did not come to greet her.

"Mother is going to be OK. Where is Pumpkin?"

"I think he is under the sofa. Probably dead. I don't smell anything. He'll come out when he is hungry."

At the sound of the can opener Pumpkin sauntered into the kitchen.

Mr. Walton looked at Pumpkin and thought viciously to himself. "Look at that snake. Walking to his food bowl when I know he is starved. Nibbling? I swear he is nibbling. He turned his butt to me, and nibbles! What the hell, I would do the same. Well, I'll be damn! He's a hard ass, stubborn, half-brained, no fear … just like me."

"Honey, Pumpkin is an OK cat. We were together for a week. His space and my space. You are so right. He will be just fine." He looked to Pumpkin and muttered, "You mafia so and so! You stay on your side of the street and I'll stay on mine!"

KING THE GROCERY KING

King was a Great Dane going on six who still retained his imaginative teenage brain. His domain was a comfortable three-bedroom house and almost an acre of St. Augustine grass bordered with azaleas, marigolds, and his favorite sunflowers. He considered it his duty to keep the mulch properly aerated along with staying on guard for suspicious acts.

Suspicious acts needed checking out. In plain sight a suspicious person who was dressed in brown and drove a brown painted truck left a suspicious brown package on the neighbor's porch. King concluded that it was an obvious ploy for an attempt to camouflage covert actions. King moved the parcel to his cabana in the back corner of his domain and covered it with a beach towel. There it stayed for five days until the evil man next door came with the secret agent in brown and carried the package off. *No finesse*.

Another package mysteriously appeared on the porch. As King went over to secure the package and place it in a safe place, he was captured. An Animal Control Officer snared him, and off he went in their truck to their animal jail. Bark, bark, bark was constant. The indoor carpeting had been removed. The ceramic water bowl was replaced with some sort of contraption on the kennel door. Everything smelled of chemical warfare. *No finesse*.

The experience left King wary of entrapments and the Animal Control vehicle. He learned the sound of it and ran into the house directly to the living room couch and peered out the window as the truck slowly drove by. He smiled at their lack of finesse. The new chain link fence was really not necessary, but it did keep out that obnoxious, bratty orange cat from God knows where.

A new strip store had opened about a mile from the house; so one Saturday King and his owners went for a walk to see if it had a pet shop. The business anchors were a grocery store on one end and a drug store on the other end. There was not a pet shop in the middle. Just as they approached the grocery store an attendant was pushing a chain of shopping carts toward the door. King playfully nudged the front cart and it veered and caught his leash out of the owner's hand. The leash and collar came free from King's neck just as the automatic doors to the grocery opened.

Naturally King rushed in. Actually he bounded. This 120-pound, black and white monster muscle with a teenage brain ran down the aisle. His tongue was out and slobbering as he raced past the cheese and dairy section. The first to go down was a stacked display of tomato soup cans…on sale, but now rolling about on the floor. He paused at the free sample stand for seafood salad. The attendant fled.

King gulped the crackers and seafood spread and winged down the wine, cola, and water section and back around past the deli to the meat counter. He inspected poultry, pork, and seafood, and settled on a four pack of sirloin strip steaks. Screams were heard in the background. Carts crashed and a handicap person in a scooter backed into a bin of cucumbers that went tumbling.

By this time the owners had King collared. They walked to the checkout line with the steaks hanging from King's drooling mouth. The manager came running and yelled "No Charge!" and waved them out.

The walk home was just as exuberant as the grocery caper. One squirrel slalomed around a fire hydrant to escape. Then it was lunch and on the couch to watch for the Animal Control vehicle.

He thought: *These humans with no finesse.*

COUGHING LITTLE BIT

Second opinions are common and often helpful in confirming a diagnosis. Because of the time lapse between each exam, clinical signs may start to appear. An example of this is the dog that was not feeling well who came in for an exam. The dog's lab work and the exam were within their normal limits; healthy dog, the first opinion. A week later an abscessed tooth became apparent to the second opinion vet when earlier it was hidden. The abscess was treated, healthy dog.

I like to encourage rechecks and second opinions. It does not bruise my ego if I miss something. I call the client back for progress reports and I also refer to or consult a specialist when needed. I was the third veterinarian to examine Little Bit for a third opinion.

His problem was coughing. I reviewed the previous x-rays, electrocardiogram, and blood work; all were within normal limits. Examination revealed no abnormalities, and I could find no reason for the cough.

The nervous owner said, "Of course he is not coughing now. You know how that happens when you go to the doctor, but believe me, he has spells of choking and hacking and coughing. It takes me an hour to calm him down!"

Little Bit sat quietly on her lap while she continued with all of the history.

Little Bit seemed rather bored and yawned.

"Put him down and let's see how he walks around and breathes."

Little Bit ran around the room in a normal manner sniffing odors and marked a vertical edge of the door with urine. I squatted to pick him up and he started to cough.

"Oh baby! Come to mama," said the owner as she held and kissed him until he stopped coughing. Little Bit gave me a knowing look as if to say, "HA! I'll piss on your door anytime." I thought about what had just happened and so I decided to try psychology.

"OK, when he wants attention he coughs. He coughs for love and you give it to him. Now, one, give him anti-anxiety meds, or, two, just love him all the time. Let's try loving first. What I am talking about is twenty-four-seven loving."

I called back in three days for an evaluation.

"Doctor, he is just fine. We spend much of our time together now. I hold him most of the day and have made a little carrier, as if he was a little baby. He also sleeps on his special pillow next to mine. I take him on walks with me twice a day. Of course he doesn't walk, so I do the walking and he sits in his carrier. It has little blue ribbons on it. He is a boy, of course you know that. He is just fine. He hasn't coughed since he peed on your door. Sorry about that. He never, never has done anything like that! Anyway thank you."

MIDNIGHT HALLOWEEN

Halloween is a time for screaming ghouls, moaning ghosts, witches riding brooms, and of course, black cats silhouetted against the moon standing on a fence.

The Halloween image of a black cat with back arched, hair bristling, ears laid back, teeth bared, and hissing as for an attack is not an aggressive cat. This cat is a fearful cat. Possibly the cat had seen a stray, ghost moaning, ghoul screaming, or it is a witch-cat with a cat wart on its cat nose, or just an afraid cat.

Another misleading craze about Halloween is that the hour of midnight is the witching hour and always a dark and black. Midnights are not always the darkest part of the night depending upon the phases of the moon, the weather, and artificial lighting. However, "midnight" could be considered a proper name for a little black kitten. And so it was, the little black kitten from the animal shelter was adopted and named, Midnight.

As Midnight matured, he was a model of propriety, even though he was of unknown ancestry. He was a little snobbish, sort of picky, sometimes finicky, and subtly fastidious. He was easy to spoil and as expected he pushed the envelope once in awhile, but never enough to start an argument. He planned his every move wisely. For example, just a little extra hesitation now and then was enough to let it be known that the litter needed freshening.

Near Halloween the Morrises, who lived next door, wanted to borrow Midnight in order to scare a "brat-kid" who lived across the street and made insulting remarks about their Chihuahua. When they would take their Chihuahua for a walk, Brat Kid would run across the street and holler things like, "That's not a dog! It's a rat with funny ears! His name must be Mickey Mouse Morris!"

The Morrises considered their neighbor's black cat to be a Halloween cat, as most superstitious humans do. The Morrises had a two-story house with a winding stairway in the entry that would be a perfect place for a Halloween scare. The neighbor and the Morrises created a master plan that involved Midnight; sure to keep Brat Kid away from their side of the street. Now Midnight was not of the temperament to be hissing at humans, but rather one of hugs and kisses, so the plan would need to be perfectly executed.

The plan was to decorate the entry to the Morris' home in a "Politically Incorrect" early Halloween theme. They would need a witch drinking blood from a punch bowl filled with floating eyeballs, a skull that nodded and blew smoke, a brain on a plate that wiggled—and much more. To pull it all together, they were going to play classical music from Bach with added moaning and groaning echoing down the staircase. Of course the entry would be dimly lit and full of spider webs.

The idea was to introduce Brat Kid to the haunted glory of this fantastic holiday. The Morrises hoped to lure him to the foot of the stairs to get candy. The scene's horror would be in full force and down would come a "bewitched" hissing black cat to the sound of Mrs. Morris's blood-curdling screams. They anticipated Brat Kid would run screaming, never to return. They practiced with Midnight, but he just sat on the stairs and nonchalantly licked his paws thinking, "How weird can humans get? I did not volunteer for this job."

The Morrises contemplated, "How are we going to get Midnight to bound down the stairs? How can we make him hiss and spit?" Mr. Morris said that they should just throw him down the stairs.

What they did not understand was that all cats have a defense mechanism. The posture of the arched back, hissing and spitting were cat body language for fear, and Midnight had never been fearful since his life was a sheltered one. He actually needed to be frightened to be frightful. There was not much hope.

Now, here come the Trick-or-Treators. Brat Kid was a pirate with an eye-patch, beard, sword, and bandana. Midnight sat on the top of the stairs bemused by all of the silly capers that humans expect the rest of the animal kingdom to find interesting. He thought that the only interest he could have in such antics was that of observing borderline insanity in the making.

When the small pirate was shoved to the foot of the stairs, Mr. Morris did a cruel thing. He stepped down hard on Midnight's tail and booted him gently down the stairs. Mrs. Morris let out her best blood-curdling scream. Midnight let out a cat scream and went hissing and bounding down the stairs and sought refuge by clinging to the pirate's sash belt with one claw while the other claw raked off the cutlass scabbard. Then up on the top of the pirate's three-corned hat he went and clung bravely.

Brat Kid, a frighten soul, fled out the door. Clinging atop his pirate's hat rode Midnight like a bareback rodeo rider. Of course, Midnight, being the more rational of the two, realized the absurdity of the situation and as soon as they passed the entry door he pushed off into the ligustrum hedge. And there he sat in solitude and meditation, secure in his superiority over imitation pirates. In the morning he sauntered back to his house, pausing every now and then to lick the dew from his pads.

It was all confusing, but harmless. Later, the story was told and re-told and embellished more and more. Now each time Brat Kid came outside, he heard nothing but the worst. Brat Kid was subjected to teasing such as "Ride'um—cat! Ride'um—hat cat rodeo!" And having been on the barbed end of mocking torments for a few days, he said very sincerely to the Morris Chihuahua, "Well, good afternoon little doggie. You're looking good today."

DAIQUIRI

Daiquiri was not feeling well. His owner said that he was depressed and not eating as much, and yet, he had a potbelly. He was a gentle cat and allowed an examination without fussing. His potbelly was not fat, but fluid collected in the abdominal cavity. The whites of his eyes were jaundice--yellow in color.

With little resistance, he let me take a blood sample and tap his abdomen for a fluid analysis. The lab work suggested "liver disease." He lay quietly while we x-rayed him. The x-ray revealed an enlarged liver, peritoneal effusion--the potbelly fluid--and no other discernable pathology.

Liver disease is a common major illness in cats and the prognosis was guarded. The owner wished to treat Daiquiri. A regimen of vitamin/mineral supplements; a healthy diet, antibiotics, and other liver medications were started. As time passed, there was some improvement. My hopes had increased because liver disease is often fatal.

Daiquiri dragged along and the blood work showed some promise, but I needed a definitive diagnosis. The owner consented to an ultrasound and a liver biopsy. The results were liver disease with toxins as a first rule out. I questioned the owner about toxic plants and every toxin I could think of. They knew of none.

Daiquiri did not return to his old playful self. The liver, however, is a remarkable organ in that it may self-cure if not abused. Each time, I would go over his life style, his diet, his water, insecticides, environment, and everything else I could imagine. No cure. He remained a droopy cat. His yellow jaundice lessened, but he was so-so.

I was driving to the animal hospital one morning and a thought zinged through my mind. How does that happen? I used to say "thank you, Dad," but it had become such a common occurrence after six years of diagnostic problem solving, that I think our sub-conscience works overtime and then … BING! Our conscience signals an idea!

I called the owner and asked, "Why is Daiquiri named *Daiquiri*?"

"Well my husband's cousin is from Daiquiri, Cuba, and he came to visit the same time we got our little Daiquiri from the animal shelter. So, we all sat around the pool drinking daiquiris and the little guy wanted some, so we let him have his cocktail. He loved it and so we named him Daiquiri. Since he was a kitten, he drinks his daiquiris in the afternoon as we all sit around the pool. He isor was before he got sicka riot when he got his buzz on. He would play with his toy mouse and his tongue would hang out and . . . ."

I interrupted and harshly said, "Do not give him anymore daiquiris! Repeat! . . . Say after me! . . . No more cocktails!"

And so it was. Over time, Daiquiri became his old playful self again, sans booze. I know he enjoyed life more so without a buzz and unaware of all the wonderful things that are unknown to alcoholics in there retreat from reality.

In fact, he was the only cat I've known who was an honorary member of FAA or Feline Alcoholic Anonymous.

BINGO THE THERAPY CAT

A cat hobbled into the manicured nursing home yard. The elderly women slowly rose from her patio rocker and kneeled over the stray.

"Well, a cat. Oh, you got grease on your fur. Hurts to move? Probably hit by a car. Don't move. I'll wrap you up in my shawl. There now, all rolled up and comfy in my lap. Some blood on your lip. Breathing O.K? Let's you and me just rock a bit. Man, did I ever rock and roll. I used to be an airline stewardess. Nowadays, they don't call them stewardess. I always had a man. Went rafting on the Colorado River and took a safari in Kenya. My men took care of me and I took care of them. There must have been maybe fifteen men. Some wanted to marry, but when you got to juke, you can't be tied down. Life is a recess, not the classroom. I broke a collarbone falling off a motorcycle. That hog--that's what they used to be called--took us across and back, all around this country. I'm worn out now. I can guarantee you that I didn't rust out. You sleep now in my shawl. Sleep tight. Don't let the bedbugs bite. They wanted me to play bingo. What a joke! Hey, Bingo is your name. How about that! A new home and a new name."

* * *

"What kind of name is Bingo? I had a cat as a boy. It used to run from me. Not you, you're a jewel. You are so warm. I'll tell you, one time when Joe and me walked down the railroad tracks, we would put a penny on the tracks and let the train flatten it out. Then, we'd go down to the trestle and throw the rocks into the river. Joe left when he was fourteen. I wonder what happened to him? Those rocks on the rail way were smooth and mostly white-like. Here comes the train! Whoo! Whoo! Are you smiling at that? Just you go and see for yourself. I'll give you directions."

* * *

"You know, Bingo, I was called Ms. Mayor. I was mayor of Greenville. We expanded our sewer system and built a public swimming pool. First lady Mayor in our history. Probably the last, too. Damn snow! Real mess! You don't know how lucky you are to be in Florida. Probably never seen snow! One time it was a blizzard. You know, folks don't squawk until the electricity is down; don't miss the water until the well runs dry. Pot holes! I swear, more complaints about potholes. People will pay more taxes just to get rid of potholes then they'll pay for the increasing of sanitation fees. Potholes, potholes. I guess I'm the pothole now."

* * *

"Dude, I had a gallstone as big as my balls. Not really, but it was a doozy! You're fixed, so I guess you don't know about sex and stuff and being together. Your way is lonely. I'll keep you company. Don't you worry? I've asked nurse to get a comb for you, maybe two combs and a brush. You shed so much! Black hair like satin. I'm bald as a cue ball! Where does all that hair come from? A little jealous you say? I wonder if anybody has made anything out of cat hair? Just the hair now, not the hide. Skinning a cat? What for? More than one way to do nothing! You winked at that, right? Smarty pants! I'll bet you don't know where the word doozy even came from. I'll tell you next time."

* * *

"I'll tell you a secret. Don't bump the glump. Never mind what a glump is. There are so many, that it defies definition. No need to fight with a fool. Just roll with it and move along. That's how come I'm ninety-two and not scarred up in the mind. My pain is the cancer that's eating me up inside. That's the secret; don't let them get inside you. You move right along, take one day at a time, and you'll be just fine. One day somebody will find a cure for this cancer, and then it'll be one cure after another. Shucks, 150 is just not worth it. I got my 90, and that's fine by me. Shortly, no more pain. At last! Pain going to go away, going, and going, gone. Lord just take me!"

* * *

"They told me you were hit by a car. Fool! You do the hitting. The people that got in my way; they got hit. Flat on their ass! Yes sir, lots of bodies. Built and developed, built more, and bribed a few. Hell paid the S.O.B.'s! Got what I wanted. It's the battle, not the war! All that B.S. Judge put me in jail. Can you believe it? She was a bitch! Probably had a sick P.M.S. day. Can you image her naked? Judge in her robe or no robe at all! What ya got? Another whore! She comes in and we all stand. My stupid heart will not let me stand anymore. Yeah, I'm a goner. I want to go to hell! Yeah, that's right; to see the bastards suffer, know what I mean? What in the hell you purring about?"

* * *

"Bingo, Bingo. Once a week I get a letter from my son, every Wednesday. He writes on a Sunday after church. I'd read it to you, but you don't understand. It's always typed in big letters, always one page, always ends with, 'LOVE YOU', in capital letters. He went over fools' hill in a quiet sort of way. I reckon he did fool things, but never told, and never argued. Always a 'yes mama'. Never married. He's a bachelor with a good government job. Bob's his name. He's going to retire next year. Said he'd move to Florida and visit me every Sunday after church. The girls don't care. Wait until this old wheelchair gets them. It don't really matter, I've got Bob, and of course, you."

* * *

"You have heard 'Once Upon a Time' stories? Well, I was the princess awaken by a kiss from a prince. O.K., it was more than a kiss. This guy was no prince and we did not live happily ever after. Do they still call it a maidenhood? He knocked me up. Do they still say that? I kept his child and lived with my aunt in Tampa until I got certified as a court recorder. I named her Jane after my aunt. Auntie Jane adopted little Janie. I moved to Miami. I was a whiz! You should have seen how my fingers moved in court. So much bad stuff people do to other people. You would not believe! Twenty some years later, guess who showed up? You guessed it. My little Janie was grown. She was a real class act. Auntie Jane had died. I introduced her to a county prosecutor. I went to their wedding. She let me care for her children. What I missed, I got back in spades. My memories are of those children. I was just skipped over a little. Don't you see? Once upon a time is real."

* * *

"Ah me, Bingo. You remind me of some of my students. The silent kind who looked attentive, but I could tell they were spinning off into their own thoughts. Learning is a trip, an odyssey. Let me tell you about an odyssey. A long time ago, the Greeks would gather for a party with entertainment. There would be a storyteller who sang a saga--an adventurous story. The stories were written down. These writings were some of the earliest forms of a novel. Homer called a collection of such, 'The Odyssey.' My trip, foray, safari is ending. I have sailed my ship into the adventures of young minds. The wonderful unfolding of my student's awareness of what they could imagine, will always stay with me. And then, there are the memories of my bride, my love. Let me sing you an odyssey:

When young Dawn with rose-red fingers comes once more,
And gilds with golden spray the lips I adore,
How to hold, horde and keep
As I draw the drapes to let my love sleep?
When aged Night with lily-pale fingers comes once more,
And shrouds with secret silence the one I adore,
Together as we sleep.

* * *

Bingo fulfilled his destiny by being a comforter with caring love for all those in the nursing home. He gave freely--a nuzzle, a smile, a wink, a purr.

INVITATION TO THE READER

I invite you to email me at: carr@bouncingballbooks.com with your impressions of my little book of short stories about the human-animal bonding relationship.

My intent is to relate the strong and important bond of love and friendship between animals and humans. Most of you probably already understand this. Please let me know.

Also, if you have experiences in your lives where animals have really made a difference to you and your family, kindly pass these stories on to me. I will appreciate and understand them.

Sincerely,

Stedman H. Carr, DVM

ANNOUNCING

NOVELS BY

STEDMAN H. CARR, DVM

"Maria, Me, and Animals"

A boy grows up in Cajun country to become a successful veterinarian in the Tampa Bay area. As he interacts with animals, the Doc learns to live life to its fullest through tragedy and joy.
2006 hard cover

"CW and Me"

A young Bostonian veterinarian accepts a position as an associate at a Kentucky equine practice. He finds himself entangled with a private horse farm where things are not what they appear to be.
2006 hard cover

"Animal Sleuths: From Doc's Mystery Files"

A student at the Veterinary College in Georgia uses his medical knowledge and animal sense to solve murder mysteries. He becomes deputized in a small town, works with the Atlanta Medical Examiner, and comes to the aide of a private investigator.
2007 hard cover

dr. ball

www.bouncingballbooks.com